The publishers are grateful for permission to reproduce the following material:

From *This the Bear and the Scary Night* by Sarah Hayes. Text Copyright © 1991 by Sarah Hayes; illustrations Copyright © 1991 by Helen Craig. By permission of Little, Brown and Company.

Reprinted with the permission of Macmillan Publishing Company from *In the Middle of the Night* by Kathy Henderson, illustrated by Jennifer Eachus. Text copyright © 1992 Kathy Henderson. Illustrations copyright © 1992 Jennifer Eachus.

Reprinted with the permission of Aladdin Books, an imprint of Macmillan Publishing from *Tom and Pippo's Day* by Helen Oxenbury. Text and illustrations copyright © 1989 Helen Oxenbury.

Published in the U.S. by Ideals Children's Books, an imprint of Hambleton-Hill Publishing, Inc, Nashville, Tennessee from *The Wish Factory* by Chris Riddell. Text and illustrations copyright © 1990 Chris Riddell.

First edition 1995

Library of Congress Cataloging-in-Publication Data is available.
Library of Congress Catalog Card Number TK.

ISBN 1-56402-652-3

2 4 6 8 10 9 7 5 3 1

Printed in Mexico

Candlewick Press
2067 Massachusetts Avenue
Cambridge, Massachusetts 02140

THE CANDLEWICK
BOOK OF
BEDTIME
STORIES

CANDLEWICK PRESS
CAMBRIDGE, MASSACHUSETTS

CONTENTS

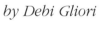

HORATIO'S BED

All night Horatio could not sleep.
He tossed and turned and
wriggled and rolled. But he
just could not get comfortable.
"I'll go and ask James what's
the matter," he thought.

James was busy drawing. Horatio sat down.
"I couldn't sleep all night," he said.
"Is it your bed?" asked James.
"I haven't got a bed," Horatio said.
"Then let's make
you one,"
said James.

by Camilla Ashforth

James took a clean sheet of paper from his Useful Box and very carefully drew a bed for Horatio. It was a big square bed with a leg at each corner.

Then he took another sheet of paper and drew another bed for Horatio. This one was a big square bed with a leg at each corner too. Horatio was very excited. He took one of James's drawings and tried to fold it into a bed.

Then he climbed inside it and closed his eyes.

It wasn't very comfortable and when Horatio rolled over . . . **RRRIIIPPP!**

James looked up. "That bed looks too hard to sleep on," he said and continued his drawing.

Horatio thought for a moment.

Then he pulled some feathers out of James's pillow and made a big square bed with them. But when he lay on it, the feathers tickled his nose.

AAACHOO!
AAACHOO!
AAACHOO!

He sneezed and sneezed. James put down his pencil and blew away the feathers.

James sat Horatio down on his Useful Box.
"You wait here a minute," he said,
"while I just finish drawing your
bed." He had already drawn five
square beds and was getting
very good at them.

But when James turned
away, Horatio slipped down
from the Useful Box. He wanted to
see what James kept inside. He made some steps up to
the lid. He pushed it open and leaned in. There were all
sorts of things—buttons, brushes, keys and clothespins,
clock wheels, clips, and little pieces of string.

Horatio looked for a bed. He couldn't
find anything that looked like
James's drawings. But he did
find a big red sock.
"Look, James!" he cried. "I've
found your other sock!"

James did not seem very
pleased. He didn't like
anyone looking in his
Useful Box. Not even Horatio.

Very quietly and carefully he started to put away his Useful Things. When he had finished, he closed the lid and looked for Horatio. "Now we can make you a bed," he said.

But there was no need, because Horatio was fast asleep. His bed was not square, and it did not have a leg at each corner.

But for little Horatio, it was just right.

A Quiet Night In

Jill Murphy

"I want you all in bed early tonight," said Mrs. Large. "It's Daddy's birthday, and we're going to have a quiet night in."

"Can we be there too?" asked Laura.

"No," said Mrs. Large. "It wouldn't be quiet with the gang of you all charging around like a herd of elephants."

"But we *are* a herd of elephants," said Lester.

"Smarty-pants," said Mrs. Large. "Come on now, coats on. It's time for school."

 That evening, Mrs. Large had the children bathed and in their pajamas before they had even had their dinner. They were all very cranky.

"It's only four-thirty," said Lester. "It's not even dark yet."

"It soon will be," said Mrs. Large grimly.

 After their baths, the children started making place cards and decorations for the dinner table. Then they all cleaned up. Then Mrs. Large cleaned up again.

Mr. Large arrived home looking very tired.

"We're all going to bed," said Lester.

"So you can be quiet," said Laura.

"Without us," said Luke.

"Shhhh," said the baby.

"Happy birthday," said Mrs. Large. "Come and see the table."

Mr. Large sank heavily into the sofa. "It's lovely, dear," he said, "but do you think we could have our dinner on trays in front of the TV? I'm feeling a little tired."

"Of course," said Mrs. Large. "It's *your* birthday. You can have whatever you want."

"We'll help," said Luke.

The children ran to the kitchen and brought two trays. "I'll set them," said Mrs. Large. "We don't want everything ending up on the floor."

"Can we have a story before we go to bed?" asked Luke.

"Please," said Lester.

"Go on, Dad," said Laura. "Just one."

"Story!" said the baby.

"Oh, all right," said Mr. Large. "Just one, then."

Lester chose a book, and they all cuddled up on the sofa.

Mr. Large opened the book and began to read: "One day Binky Bus drove out of the big garage. 'Hello!' he called to his friend, Micky Milktruck—"

"I don't like that one," said Laura. "It's a boy's story."

"Look," said Mr. Large, "if you're going to argue about it, you can all go straight to bed without *any* story."

So they sat and listened while Mr. Large read to them.

After a while he stopped.

"Go on, Daddy," said Luke. "What happened after he bumped into Gary Garbagetruck?"

"Did they have a fight?" asked Lester.

"Look," said Laura. "Daddy's asleep."

"Shhhh!" said the baby.

Mrs. Large laughed. "Poor Daddy," she said.
"Never mind, we'll let him snooze a little longer
while I take you all up to bed."
"Will you just finish the story, Mom?" asked Lester.
"We don't know what happens in the end," said Luke.
"Please," said Laura.
"Story!" said the baby.

 "Move over, then," said Mrs. Large.
She picked up the book and began to read:
"'Watch where you're going, you silly
Garbagetruck!' said Binky. Just then, Patty
the Police Car came driving by . . ."
After a while, Mrs. Large stopped reading.

18

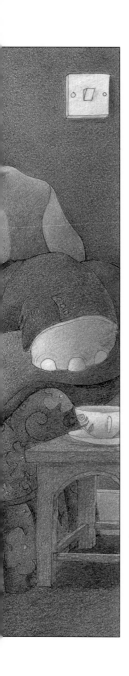

"What's that strange noise?" asked Lester.
"It's Mommy snoring," said Luke. "Daddy's
snoring too."
"They must be very tired," said Laura, kindly.
"Shhhh!" said the baby.
The children crept from the sofa and got a
blanket. They covered Mr. and Mrs. Large
and tucked them in.

"We'd better put ourselves to bed," said Lester.
"Come on."
"Should we take the food up with us?" asked
Luke. "It *is* on trays."
"It's a pity to waste it," said Laura. "I'm sure
they wouldn't mind. Anyway, they wanted
a quiet night in."
"Shhhh!" said the baby.

What Is the Sun?

Reeve Lindbergh
illustrated by Stephen Lambert

What is the sun?
The sun is a star.

Is the sun near?
No, it is far.

What does it do?
It sends light down to you.

Like my lamp, only higher?
More like a big fire.

Can I see it at night?
No, you see the moonlight.

The moon is a star?
Not a star, just a place.

What else does it do?
It pulls the tides, too.

What are the tides?
The whole moving sea.

With the fish, and the whales?
Yes, definitely.

Why does it smile?
It looks like a face.

Where do tides go?
Up and down, ebb and flow.

Sometimes thin, sometimes fat?
Yes, the moon is like that.

On the beach where I play?
Up and down, night and day.

Does it shine in the day?
No, it just fades away.

Tides go out and go in?
Like your breath, and the wind.

What is the rain?
The rain makes things grow.

Like the flowers and trees?
And the rivers that flow.

Where does it rain?
On the sea, hill, and plain.

And it rains on my head?
Not when you're here in bed!

And after the rain?
Then the earth's green again.

What is the wind?
Wind is air, blowing air.

Where does it blow?
Through the world, everywhere.

The wind comes and goes?
It goes right through your nose!

But that can be cold!
When deep winter takes hold.

Is wind ever warm?
In a summer rainstorm.

22

What is the earth?
It's our home—a big ball.

With the sun and the moon?
And the raindrops that fall.

And the wind and the tides?
And the people, besides.

Even children, like me?
Everybody you see.

So you'll be here too?
Yes, forever, with you.

Then I think it's all right
I love you. . . . Good night.

Good Night, Lily

Martha Alexander

No more read. Lily sleepy.

Now Willy read. Look, Teddy.

Now Willy sleepy.

TOM AND PIPPO'S DAY

Helen Oxenbury

When I wake up early in the morning, first I give Pippo a hug, then we go to see if Mommy and Daddy are awake. Daddy has to hurry with his breakfast.

Sometimes I give
Pippo some of mine,
but he's so clumsy
and he makes a mess.

Pippo and I do things
together all day,
until Daddy
comes home.

When it's bedtime, sometimes I don't
know where Pippo is and I have to
look everywhere
until I find him.

Because when it's time
to go to sleep, I need
to be with Pippo.

29

THE WISH FACTORY

Chris Riddell

Oliver used to have a
bad dream about a monster.
But one night a cloud came
instead of the dream . . .

and carried Oliver into the big blue
night—far, far away to the Wish Factory.

Oliver closed his eyes
and thought a big wish.
Then the wishmakers made
it good and strong . . .

and wrapped it up to keep it fresh.

"We hope it comes true," they said.

Then Oliver was in his own bed
and dreaming . . .

THE BIG BAD DREAM.

So Oliver untied the ribbon
and out came the wish . . .

and the wish came true.

The monster wasn't big anymore,
and it wasn't bad. "BOO!" said Oliver.

And morning
came very soon.

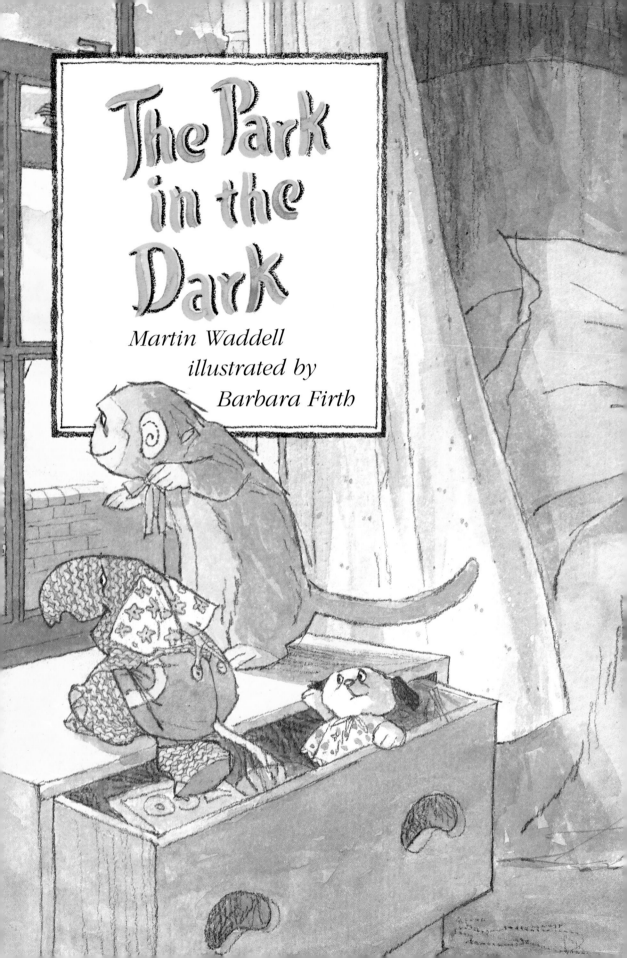

The Park in the Dark

Martin Waddell

illustrated by

Barbara Firth

When the sun goes down
and the moon comes up
and the old swing creaks
in the dark,
that's when we go to the park,
   me and Loopy
      and Little Gee,
        all three.

Softly down the staircase,
through the haunty hall,
trying to look small,
   me and Loopy
      and Little Gee,
        we three.

It's shivery
out in the dark
on our way to the park,
down trash can alley,
past the ruined mill,
so still,
   just me and Loopy
      and Little Gee,
        just three.

And Little Gee doesn't like it.
He's scared of the things he might see
in the park in the dark
with Loopy and me.
    That's me and Loopy
        and Little Gee,
            the three.

There might be moon witches
or man-eating trees
or withers that wobble
or old Scrawny Shins
or hairy hobgoblins
or black boggarts' knees in the trees
or things we can't see,
    me and Loopy
        and little Gee,
            all three.

But there aren't, says Loopy,
 and I agree,
and Little Gee gets up on my back
and we pass the Howl Tree,
    me and Loopy
        and Little Gee.
            We're heroes, we three.

In the park in the dark
by the lake and the bridge,
at last we see
where we want to be,
 me and Loopy
  and Little Gee.
   WHOOPEE!

And we swing and we slide
and we dance and we jump
and we chase all over the place,
 me and Loopy
  and Little Gee,
   the Big Three!

And then the THING comes!
*YAAAAA AAAIII
OOOOOEEEEEE!*

RUN RUN RUN!
shouts Little Gee
to Loopy and me
and we flee,
    me and Loopy
        and Little Gee,
            scared three.

Back where we came
through the park in the dark
and the THING is roaring
and following, see?
    After me and Loopy
        and Little Gee,
            we three.

Up to the house, to the stair,
to the bed where we ought to be,
me and Loopy
and Little Gee,
safe as can be,
all three.

◇ TEN IN THE BED ◇
Penny Dale

There were ten in the bed

and the little one said, "Roll over, roll over!"
So they all rolled over and Hedgehog fell out . . .

BUMP!

There were nine in the bed
and the little one said,
"Roll over, roll over!"
So they all rolled over
and Zebra fell out . . .

OUCH!

There were eight in the bed
and the little one said,
"Roll over, roll over!"
So they all rolled over
and Ted fell out . . .

THUMP!

There were seven in the bed
and the little one said,
"Roll over, roll over!"
So they all rolled over
and Croc fell out . . .

THUD!

There were four in the bed
and the little one said,
"Roll over, roll over!"
So they all rolled over
and Nellie fell out . . .

CRASH!

There were six in the bed
and the little one said,
"Roll over, roll over!"
So they all rolled over
and Rabbit fell out . . .

BONK!

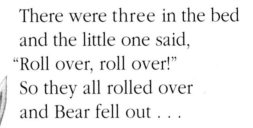

There were three in the bed
and the little one said,
"Roll over, roll over!"
So they all rolled over
and Bear fell out . . .

SLAM!

There were five in the bed
and the little one said,
"Roll over, roll over!"
So they all rolled over
and Mouse fell out . . .

PLINK!

There were two in the bed
and the little one said,
"Roll over, roll over!"
So they all rolled over
and Sheep fell out . . .

PLONK!

43

There was one in the bed
and the little one said,
"I'm cold! I miss you!"

So they all came back and jumped into bed—
Hedgehog, Mouse, Nellie, Zebra, Ted, the little one, Rabbit, Croc,
Bear, and Sheep.

Ten in the bed,
all fast asleep.

Jan Ormerod

MIDNIGHT PILLOW FIGHT

Have *you* ever woken up in the middle of the night?
Have *you* ever had a midnight pillow fight?

Polly has . . . and look how it started.

Polly thought her pillow was alive.
She thought it wanted to play.

Has *your* pillow ever wanted to
play in the middle of the night?

Polly's has.

Look, they went downstairs on tiptoe.

Polly peeked and what did she see?
Some cushions were awake too.

For a moment Polly stood and watched.
I wonder what she felt, don't you?

This is how Polly said hello.
And this is how they played.

Now where did these big
cushions come from?

Have *you* ever marched
and danced like this,
having lots of fun in the
middle of the night?

47

Look, they played leapfrog.

Up and over . . .

up and over . . .

up and over!

BUMP! Oh, poor pillow!

Polly pushed—would *you* do that? Polly got ready to fight.

Ready, steady . . .

WHOOSH! WALLOP!

WHOOSH! WHOP!

WHOOSH! WHOP!

WALLOP!

"Please stop!"
Polly turned on the light.

And the pillow
fight stopped.

Polly put the
cushions back in
their places.

Everything was
still again.

Polly took her
pillow up to bed.

Why do you
think she
looked so sad?

Have *you* ever hugged your pillow in the middle of the night? Polly has.
And look! All the cushions came upstairs to see if Polly was all right.

Have *you* ever
woken up in
the middle of
the night?

Have *you*
ever had a
midnight
pillow fight?

Polly has . . .
and this is
how it ended.

THIS IS THE BEAR AND THE SCARY NIGHT

Sarah Hayes illustrated by Helen Craig

This is the boy
who forgot his bear
and left him behind
in the park on a chair.

Bye-bye!

This is the bear
who looked at the moon
and hoped the boy
would come back soon.

This is the bear
alone in the park.
And these are the eyes that
glowed in the dark.

This is the owl who
swooped down in the night
and gave the bear
a terrible fright.

This is the bear
up in the sky.
This is the owl
who struggled to fly.

These are the claws
that couldn't hold on.
And this is the bear who
fell . . . into . . . the pond.

This is the bear
who floated all night.
This is the dark that
turned into light.

This is the man
with the slide trombone
who rescued the bear
and took him home.

Out you come.

This is the bear
in a warm blue sweater
who made a friend
and felt much better.

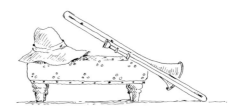

I've been out
all night!

That's my sweater.

This is the boy
who remembered his bear
and ran to the park
and found him there.

This is the bear
who started to tell
how he flew through the
air and how he fell . . .

and how he floated
and how he was saved
and how he was
terribly, terribly brave.

And this is the boy
who grinned and said,
"I know a bear
who is ready for bed."

Bounce Bounce Bounce

A Lap Game Poem

Kathy
Henderson

illustrated by
Carol Thompson

Chairs are for sitting on.
Bounce bounce bounce!

Beds are for lying on.
Dance dance dance!

Teddies are for cuddling.
Up in the air and down!

And clothes are for putting on.
Round and round and round!

Saucepans are for cooking in.
Crash crash crash!

Water is for washing with.
Splash splash splash!

Cribs are for sleeping in.
Squeak squeak squeak!

And parents, what are parents for?
Sleep sleep sleep!

A BIG DAY FOR Little Jack

Inga Moore

party and some new shoes for him to wear.

"Now we will buy you a jacket," said Daddy. "You must dress up if you are going to a party."

Little Jack Rabbit had never been to a party before. He had never had to dress up.

"Will *you* come with me?" he asked. "Will *you* come to the party?"

"Daddies aren't invited, Little Jack," said Daddy.

One day the mailman brought a card for Little Jack Rabbit.

Mommy read it out loud. It said, "You are invited to a party." Little Jack had never been to a party before.

"Will you come with me?" he asked.

"Mommies aren't invited, Little Jack," said Mommy.

Little Jack Rabbit went shopping with Daddy. They bought a present for Little Jack to take to the

At home Little Jack Rabbit's sisters Nancy, Rhona, and Rita wrapped up the present in some blue-and-white-striped paper. "Don't forget to take it to the party, Little Jack," said Nancy.

Little Jack Rabbit had never
been to a party before.
He had never had to dress
up and he had never taken
a present.
"Will *you* come with me?"
he asked.
"Big sisters aren't invited,
Little Jack," said Nancy.

Before the party Little Jack
Rabbit's big brother Buck
gave him a hot soapy bath.
Buck had been to lots
of parties.
"What are parties
like?" asked Little
Jack.
"You'll play party
games," said
Buck, "and
make new
friends."
Little Jack Rabbit
had never been to
a party before. He
had never had to
dress up and he
had never taken
a present. He had
never played party

games or made
new friends.
"Will *you* come
with me?" he
asked.
"Big brothers
aren't invited,
Little Jack,"
said Buck.

Granpa had been fixing
a toy for Little Jack Rabbit.
It was Little Jack's favorite
toy, Bunnikin.
"Why aren't you ready,
Little Jack?" Granpa asked.
"You will be late for
the party."
"I don't want to go," said
Little Jack Rabbit.
"Why not?" asked Granpa.
"I don't want to go by
myself," said Little Jack.
"Why don't you go with
Bunnikin?" asked Granpa.
"Are Bunnikins invited?"
asked Little Jack Rabbit.
"Oh, yes," said Granpa,
"I should think so, Little
Jack. I should think
Bunnikins are invited."

So Little Jack Rabbit put on his fancy new jacket and his shiny new shoes and he went to the party with Bunnikin.

Little Jack Rabbit held on to Bunnikin. He played Red Light, Green Light and Ring-Around-the-Rosy. But when he tried to play Hot Potato he had to leave Bunnikin on the ground—and when he came back, what did he find . . .

them together," said Rosy. "Come on, let's go have some cake."

After the cake Little Jack Rabbit had so much fun playing with his new friend Rosy that he didn't want to go home when Granpa came to get him.

"Don't forget Bunnikin, Little Jack," said Granpa.

but a teddy sitting next to Bunnikin. The teddy belonged to Rosy.

"I've never been to a party before," said Rosy.
"Is that why you brought Teddy?" asked Little Jack Rabbit.
"Yes," said Rosy.
"I brought Bunnikin," said Little Jack.
"I think Teddy likes Bunnikin," said Rosy.
"Bunnikin likes Teddy," said Little Jack.
"Maybe we should leave

It had been a big day for
Little Jack Rabbit. He had
been to his first party.

"I'm going to another party
soon," said Little Jack.
"Oh," said Mommy.
"It's Rosy's party," said
Little Jack.

"Can I come with you?"
asked Mommy.
"No," said Little Jack.
"But I'm your mommy,"
said Mommy.
"Mommies aren't invited,"
said Little Jack Rabbit.
"Good night, Little Jack,"
said Mommy.

Can't You Sleep, Little Bear?

Martin Waddell • illustrated by Barbara Firth

Once there were two bears. Big Bear and Little Bear. Big Bear is the big bear, and Little Bear is the little bear. They played all day in the bright sunlight. When night came, and the sun went down, Big Bear took Little Bear home to the Bear Cave.

Big Bear put Little Bear to bed in the dark part of the cave. "Go to sleep, Little Bear," he said. And Little Bear tried. Big Bear settled in the Bear Chair and read his Bear Book by the light of the fire. But Little Bear couldn't get to sleep.

"Can't you sleep, Little Bear?" asked Big Bear, putting down his Bear Book (which was just getting to the interesting part) and padding over to the bed. "I'm scared," said Little Bear. "Why are you scared, Little Bear?" asked Big Bear. "I don't like the dark," said Little Bear. "What dark?" said Big Bear. "The dark all around us," said Little Bear.

Big Bear looked, and he saw that the dark part of the cave was very dark, so he went to the Lantern Cupboard and took out the tiniest lantern that was there. Big Bear lit the tiniest lantern and put it next to Little Bear's bed. "There's a tiny light to stop you from being scared, Little Bear," said Big Bear. "Thank you, Big Bear," said Little Bear, cuddling up in the glow. "Now go to sleep, Little Bear," said Big

Bear, and he padded back to the Bear Chair and settled down to read the Bear Book by the light of the fire.

Little Bear tried to go to sleep, but he couldn't.

"Can't you sleep, Little Bear?" yawned Big Bear, putting down his Bear Book (with just four pages to go to the interesting bit) and padding over to the bed. "I'm scared," said Little Bear. "Why are you scared, Little Bear?" asked Big Bear. "I don't like the dark," said Little Bear. "What dark?" asked Big Bear. "The dark all around us," said Little Bear.

"But I brought you a lantern!" said Big Bear. "Only a teeny-weeny one," said Little Bear. "And there's lots of dark!"

Big Bear looked, and he saw that Little Bear was quite right. There was still lots of dark. So Big Bear went to the Lantern Cupboard and took out a bigger lantern. Big Bear lit the lantern and put it beside the other one.

"Now go to sleep, Little Bear," said Big Bear, and he padded back to the Bear Chair and settled down to read the Bear Book by the light of the fire.

Little Bear tried and tried to go to sleep, but he couldn't.

"Can't you sleep, Little Bear?" grunted Big Bear, putting down his Bear Book (with just three pages to go) and padding over to the bed.

"I'm scared," said Little Bear. "Why are you scared, Little Bear?" asked Big Bear. "I don't like the dark," said Little Bear. "What dark?" asked Big Bear. "The dark all around us," said Little Bear. "But I brought you two lanterns!" said Big Bear. "A tiny one and a bigger one!" "Not much bigger," said Little Bear. "And there's still lots of dark."

Big Bear thought about it, and then he went to the Lantern Cupboard and took out the Biggest Lantern of Them All, with two handles and a piece of chain. He hooked up the lantern above Little Bear's bed. "I've brought you the Biggest Lantern of Them All!" he told Little Bear. "That's to keep you from being scared!" "Thank you, Big Bear," said Little Bear, curling up in the glow and watching the shadows dance.

"Now go to sleep, Little Bear," said Big Bear, and he padded back to the Bear Chair and settled down to read the Bear Book by the light of the fire.

Little Bear tried and tried and tried to go to sleep, but he couldn't.

"Can't you sleep, Little Bear?" groaned Big Bear, putting down his Bear Book (with just two pages to go) and padding over to the bed. "I'm scared," said Little Bear. "Why are you scared, Little Bear?" asked Big Bear. "I don't like the dark," said Little Bear. "What dark?" asked Big Bear. "The dark all around us," said Little Bear. "But I brought you the Biggest Lantern of Them All, and there isn't any dark left," said Big Bear. "Yes, there is!" said Little Bear. "There is. Out there!" And he pointed out of the Bear Cave at the night.

Big Bear saw that Little Bear was right. Big Bear was very puzzled. All the lanterns in the world couldn't light up the dark outside. Big Bear thought about it for a long time, and then he said, "Come on, Little Bear." "Where are we going?" asked Little Bear. "Out!" said Big Bear. "Out into the darkness?" said Little Bear. "Yes!" said Big Bear. "But I'm scared of the dark!" said Little Bear. "No need to be!" said Big Bear, and he took Little Bear by the paw and led him out of the cave into the night and it was . . . DARK!

"Ooooh! I'm scared," said Little Bear, cuddling up to Big Bear. Big Bear lifted Little Bear and cuddled him and said, "Look at the dark, Little Bear." And Little Bear looked. "I've brought you the moon, Little Bear," said Big Bear.

"The bright yellow moon and all the twinkly stars."

But Little Bear didn't say anything, for he had gone to sleep, warm and safe in Big Bear's arms. Big Bear carried Little Bear back into the Bear Cave, fast asleep, and he settled down with Little Bear on one arm and the Bear Book on the other, cozy in the Bear Chair by the fire.

And Big Bear read the Bear Book right to . . .

THE END

◇ TEN OUT OF BED ◇

 There  were ten

Penny Dale

 out  of  bed ...

and the little one said, "Let's play!"
And Hedgehog said, "Let's play **TRAINS!**"

So they
all played
trains until
Hedgehog
fell asleep.

There were nine out of bed and the little one said, "Let's play!"
And Ted said, "Let's play **BEACHES!**"

So nine
played
beaches
until Ted
fell asleep.

There were eight out of bed and the little one said, "Let's play!"
And Rabbit said, "Let's play **ACTING!**"

So eight
played
acting
until Rabbit
fell asleep.

There were seven out of bed and the little one said, "Let's play!"
And Bear said, "Let's play **PIRATES!**"

So seven
played
pirates
until Bear
fell asleep.

There were six out of bed and the little one said, "Let's play!"
And Sheep said, "Let's play **DANCING!**"

So six
played
dancing
until Sheep
fell asleep.

There were five out of bed and the little one said, "Let's play!"
And Croc said, "Let's play **GHOSTS!**"

So five
played
ghosts
until Croc
fell asleep.

There were four out of bed and the little one said, "Let's play!"
And Nellie said, "Let's play **FLYING!**"

So four
played
flying
until Nellie
fell asleep.

There were three out of bed and the little one said, "Let's play!"
And Zebra said, "Let's play **CAMPING!**"

So three
played
camping
until Zebra
fell asleep.

There were two out of bed and the little one said, "Let's play!"
And Mouse said, "Let's play **MONSTERS!**"

So two
played
Monsters
until Mouse
fell asleep.

There was one out of bed and the little one said,
"I'm sleepy now!"

So he slipped under the covers next to Ted.
Good night, sweet dreams,

. . . ten in the bed.

When I'm BIG
Debi Gliori

What are you doing up? It's way past your bedtime.

But I'm not sleepy.

Oh yes, you are. I'll tuck you in.

It's no fun being little . . . I wish I were big. One day I will be big and . . .

When I'm big, I'm going to stay up as late as I want and make myself marshmallows on toast instead of going to bed.

When I'm big, I'm going swimming with the whales in the deep blue sea instead of splashing around in the bathtub.

When I'm big, I'm going to wear a bird suit and boots all day long instead of a sweater and jeans.

When I'm big, I'm going to have a huge backyard with sand mountains that touch the sky and a lake in the middle instead of a sandbox and a wading pool.

When I'm big, I'm going to drive the shopping cart around the store with you in it instead of the other way around.

When I'm big, I'm going to grow Venus flytraps and man-eating orchids instead of parsley and beans.

When I'm big, I'm going to ride a real bike instead of a tricycle.

When I'm big, I'm going to have twelve lions, two tigers, a bunch of grizzly bears, and a shark instead of a dog, a cat, and a goldfish.

When I'm big, I'm going to put you and Mom to bed and read you a story and turn out the light and go downstairs on my own.

GO TO BED!

Virginia Miller

It was time for Bartholomew to go to bed.

"Ba, time for bed," George said.

"Nah!" said Bartholomew.

George said, "Brush your teeth and go to bed."

"Nah!" said Bartholomew.

"Have you brushed your teeth yet, Ba?"

"Nah!" said Bartholomew, beginning to cry.

"Come on, Ba, into bed!" George said.

"Nah!" said Bartholomew. "Nah, nah, nah, nah, NAH!" said Bartholomew.

85

Go to bed

George said in
a big voice.
Bartholomew
got into bed.

He giggled
and wriggled,
he hid
and tiggled,
he cuddled
and huggled,
he snuggled
and sighed.

"Good night,
Bartholomew,"
said George.

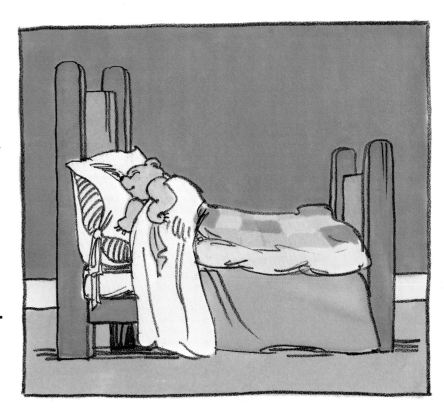

Nah said
Bartholomew
softly.

He gave a big
yawn, closed
his eyes, and
went to sleep.

IN THE MIDDLE OF THE NIGHT

Kathy Henderson
illustrated by Jennifer Eachus

A long time after bedtime

when it's very very late

when even dogs dream

and there's deep sleep

breathing through the house

when the doors are locked

and the curtains drawn

and the shops are dark

and the last train's gone

and there's no more traffic

in the street

because everyone's asleep

then

the window cleaner comes

to the main street shop fronts

and polishes the glass

in the street-lit dark

and a big truck rumbles past

on its way to the dump

loaded with the last

of the old day's trash.

On the twentieth floor

of the office tower

there's a lighted window

and high up there

another night cleaner's

vacuuming the floor

working nights on her own

while her children sleep at home.

And down in the dome of the
  observatory
the astronomer who's waited all day
  for the dark
is watching the good black sky at last

for stars and moons
and spikes of light
through her telescope
in the middle of the night
while everybody sleeps.

and out by the gate

rows of parked vans wait

for their drivers to come

and take the newly baked

bread to the shops

for the time when the

bread eaters wake.

Across the town at the hospital

where the nurses watch in the

  dim-lit wards

someone very old shuts their eyes

and dies

breathes their very last breath

on their very last night.

At the bakery

the bakers in their floury clothes

mix dough in machines

for tomorrow's loaves of bread

Yet not far away on another floor

after months of waiting

a new baby's born

and the mother and the father

hold the baby and smile

and the baby looks up

and the world's just begun

but still everybody sleeps.

Now through the silent station

past the empty shops

and the office towers

past the sleeping streets

and the hospital

a train with no windows

goes rattling by

and inside the train the sorters sift

urgent letters and packets on the

　late night shift

so tomorrow's mail will arrive in time

at the towns and the villages

　down the line.

And the mother

with the wakeful child in her arms

walking up and down

and up and down

and up and down

the room

hears the train as it passes by

and the cats in the yard

and the night owl's flight

and hums hushabye and hushabye

we should be asleep now

you and I

it's late and time to close your eyes

it's the middle of the night.